Ahoy, mateys! Do you want to join my pirate crew? Then just say the pirate password: "Yo-ho-ho!" As part of my crew, you'll need to learn the Never Land pirate pledge.

TODAY'S PIRATE PLEDGE

A good pirate always shares with his mateys.

DISNEP PRESS

First Edition
ISBN 978-1-4231-6392-3

J689-1817-1-13088

Manufactured in the USA
For more Disney Press fun, visit www.disneybooks.com

SUSTAINABLE
FORESTRY
INITIATIVE

Certified Chain of Custody
Promoting Sustainable Forestry

www.sfiprogram.org
SFI-01415

The SFI label applies to the text stock

X MARKS THE CROC!

WRITTEN BY MELINDA LAROSE

BASED ON THE EPISODE "ROCK THE CROC" BY
NICOLE DUBUC

ILLUSTRATED BY ALAN BATSON

DISNEP PRESS
New York

The sun is shining on Pirate Island.

Jake spots something in the  water.

" Treasure ahoy, mateys!"

It's a message in a bottle from Peter Pan!

4

"A  of Pirates' Plunge!" says Cubby.
"Pirates' Plunge is the coolest waterslide in all of Never Land," says Jake.
"Yo-ho, let's go!" says Izzy.

Can you find Bucky on the map?

"There's  Jake and his crew," says  Hook.

"Where are they going?"

"The  map said Pirates' Plunge is this way," calls  Cubby.

"Pirates' Plunge?" asks .
Hook
"Of course! Those puny pirates
are going to cool off on the ⟨waterslide⟩.
⟨Smee⟩, I want that ⟨map⟩!"

7

How many coconuts can you find on the beach?

Yoink!  nabs the 🗺️.
Hook   map

"Yay-hey, no way!" shouts 👧.
                                    Izzy

"Don't swipe our 🗺️," says 👦.
                          map   Jake

"Let's go to Pirates' Plunge together!"

8

"Together? Never!" says .
Hook
"I want the place all to myself!"
 tries to grab the back.
Jake   bottle
It goes flying into the sky!

9

"Shiver me timbers," says  Izzy.

"The croc ate the map!"

"Aww, coconuts!" says Cubby. "Now no one can go to Pirates' Plunge."

Just then, a  feather lands on Cubby's nose.

"Ahh…ahhh…CHOO!"

"That's it!" says Jake. "We can get the croc to sneeze out the map!"

11

Can you help Jake spot the crocodile?

The crew finds the sleeping.
croc

"Maybe he will sneeze if we tickle

his nose with a 🪶," says 🧑.
feather   Jake

"Worked for me," says 🧒.
                          Cubby

AHH
AHH
AHH

 tickles the  nose.
Skully   croc's

"Ahh…ahhh…ahhh…"

"Get set to catch the ," says .
                                    map   Jake

But the  doesn't sneeze!
         croc

"Step aside, silly swabs," says .

Hook

He rubs a feather on the croc's nose.

"Gootchy-gootchy-goo!"

But the croc doesn't sneeze!

"Why didn't it work, Smee?"

 asks.

"I don't…ahhh…ahhh…CHOO!"

 sneezes and wakes up the !

15

"Save me,  !" yells  .
Smee   Hook

He runs off.

Just then,  and  hear a burp.
Jake   Izzy

"Excuse me," says  .
Cubby

"Great thinking, ," says  .
Cubby   Izzy

BURP!

"Maybe we can make the  croc

burp out the  map ," says  Jake .

"The fizzy  water at Geyser Gulch

makes me burp," says  Izzy .

"Hey,  croc , want a drink of  water ?"

"The  sure is drinking a lot of
_{croc}

that fizzy ," says .
_{water}   _{Izzy}

"Look out! He's going to blow!"

warns .
_{Skully}

18

"Get set to catch the ," says .
map Jake
The  lets out a teeny-tiny burp.
croc
"That's it?" says .
Cubby

BURP!!

19

How many gushing geysers do you see?

"I'll make the  burp," says .
croc   Hook

 pats the  tummy, but
Hook   croc's

the  doesn't like it one bit.
croc

The  sends  flying!
croc   Hook

20

"Smeeeeeee!" yells .
Hook

"Flap your arms, Cap'n," says .
Smee

"Always works for me," says .
Skully

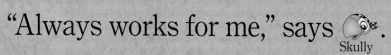 giggles at joke.
Cubby   Skully's

", you're full of ideas," says .

Cubby   Jake

"I am?" asks .

Cubby

"Maybe we can make the  laugh

croc

out the ," says .

map   Jake

22

"A ha-ha-ha and hee-hee-hee.

Come on,  croc, and laugh with me!"

"Crackers! He's not even cracking

a smile," says  Skully.

"I'll show you how it's done,"
says .
 clowns around, but the
still doesn't laugh.

What colors do you see on Hook's clown suit?

24

"Give me my crocodile ," yells . "I want that !"
Hook   map
"We all want the ," says ,
                 map   Jake
"but trapping the  isn't right."
                  croc

25

", a little ⬤, please," says 🧑.
Izzy   Pixie Dust   Jake

🧑 takes the 🥅 from 🐻.
Jake   net   Smee

"Give me back my 🥅!" yells 👒.
net   Hook

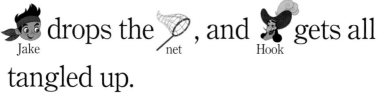 drops the , and gets all tangled up.

"Uh-oh, sorry, ," says  .

27

"Get me out of this net!" calls Hook.

He steps on a log.

The croc hits the log, and Hook goes flying. "Whoooooaaaa!"

"The croc is laughing!" says Jake.
The bottle with the map flies out of
the croc's mouth.
"Yo-ho, way to go!" says Jake.

29

Can you spot
Captain Hook and
Mr. Smee?

" was right! Pirates' Plunge is
Peter Pan
awesome!" says .
Cubby
"Too bad  tried to swipe our ,"
Hook   map
says .
Izzy

30

"If that sneaky snook had shared,
he would be in the  water instead
of up a  tree ," says  Izzy .

"For solving pirate problems,
we earned some Gold Doubloons!"

says .
Jake

"Yay-hey, well done," says 🏴‍☠️.
Izzy

How many Gold
Doubloons did Ja[ke]
and the cre[w]
earn[?]